Dedication

For William, Anna, and Autumn

Westside Storybooks

Text copyright 2020 by Katie Setterberg
Pictures copyright 2020 by Morgan Thomason

Author Information at www.westsidestorybooks.com and @westsidestorybooks
Illustrator Information at www.etsy.com/shop/WinsomePaperGoods and @winsomepaper

On the day you were born,
right from the start,

A new kind of love
took root in my heart.

Your hands and your feet,
your eyes and your nose,

I loved you completely
from your head to your toes.

Each new day you grew more
than ever before.

And you learned that the world was yours to explore.

And soon you were walking and spreading your wings.

And I loved your delight

in the simplest things.

Like the woosh of the wind
through the wild willow trees.

And the soft buzzing sound
Of sweet honeybees.

10/28 —

12/2 —

8/10 —
8/2 —

7/2 —

3/17 —

12/21 —

And as I stood watching
each part of you grow,

I loved you completely
from your head to your toes.

Days seemed to pass quickly.

In the blink of an eye,

It was time to start school,

and your bus had arrived.

You climbed that big step,
and called out, "Goodbye!"

Though my heart skipped a beat,
I knew you'd be fine.

You had all you needed
stored up safe inside.

You were not only smart,
but friendly and kind.

And soon you were learning
math, reading, and prose,

And I loved you completely
from your head to your toes.

The months turned into years,
you learned many new things.

Such as how to
work hard,

and the thrill
success brings.

You learned things can be tough,
the sting of defeat.

How alongside the joy,
sometimes there is grief.

Graduation day came.
You put on your robe,

Both nervous and eager
for life to unfold.

I looked on in wonder
at how much you'd grown,

And I loved you completely
from your head to your toes.

I don't know what is next,
where life's journey will lead,

But I hope that you know
you're loved and you're free.

So, I'll leave you with this,
these words I bestow...

Whatever may come,
wherever you go,

I love you completely
from your head to your toes.

CPSIA information can be obtained
at www.ICGtesting.com
Printed in the USA
BVHW021807291020
592147BV00013B/91